Chicks Rule!

STORY BY
Sudipta Bardhan-Quallen

PICTURES BY
Renée Kurilla

Abrams Books for Young Readers • New York

ROCKET CLUB
THE COOLEST CLUB IN THE GALAXY
MEETING TODAY
NO CHICKS ALLOWED!!!

Cool chicks and nerdy chicks
Quiet chicks and wordy chicks

Biker chicks and rocker chicks
Science chicks and soccer chicks

Coding chicks and gaming chicks

Bow-and-arrow-aiming chicks

Chicks who draw and chicks who read
Chicks who follow, chicks who lead

Chicks all travel separate roads

Chicks all carry different loads

Hippie chicks and baker chicks

Yoga chicks and maker chicks

Army chicks and sailor chicks

Sporty chicks and tailor chicks

Writer chicks and chicks who teach
Surfer chicks and chicks who preach

Chicks arrive from all directions
Nearing the same intersection

Though they've followed separate tracks

A common hurdle holds them back

But chicks are strong and chicks are smart
Chicks have guts and chicks have heart
To find this problem's best solution
Each chick must make contributions

Chicks suggest and chicks devise
Chicks find ways to compromise

Chicks reflecting

Chicks conceiving

Chicks producing

Chicks believing

Soon chicks of different flocks and feathers
Work to reach the stars together

With delight and jubilation

Chicks move toward their destination

And though their journeys will proceed

Chicks have learned they WILL succeed

All in step with wing in wing . . .

Chicks can conquer
anything!

To all our daughters, who will succeed.
—S. B. Q.

For all the brave, persistent chicks who aim high.
You got this!
—R. K.

This book was sketched, penciled, and painted entirely in Adobe Photoshop.

Cataloging-in-Publication Data has been applied for and
may be obtained from the Library of Congress.

ISBN 978-1-4197-3414-4

Text copyright © 2019 Sudipta Bardhan-Quallen
Illustrations copyright © 2019 Renée Kurilla
Book design by Pamela Notarantonio

Printed and bound in China
10 9 8 7 6 5 4 3 2 1

Abrams Books for Young Readers are available at special discounts when
purchased in quantity for premiums and promotions as well as fundraising or
educational use. Special editions can also be created to specification.
For details, contact specialsales@abramsbooks.com or the address below.

Abrams® is a registered trademark of Harry N. Abrams, Inc.

ABRAMS The Art of Books
195 Broadway, New York, NY 10007
abramsbooks.com